Welcome to ALADDIN QUIX!

If you are looking for fast, fun-to-read stories with colorful characters, lots of kid-friendly humor, easy-to-follow action, entertaining story lines, and lively illustrations, then **ALADDIN QUIX** is for you!

But wait, there's more!

If you're also looking for stories with tables of contents; word lists; about-the-book questions; 64, 80, or 96 pages; short chapters; short paragraphs; and large fonts, then **ALADDIN QUIX** is *definitely* for you!

ALADDIN QUIX: The next step between ready to reads and longer, more challenging chapter books, for readers five to eight years old.

Read more ALADDIN QUIX books!

By Stephanie Calmenson

Our Principal Is a Frog!
Our Principal Is a Wolf!
Our Principal's in His Underwear!
Our Principal Breaks a Spell!
Our Principal's Wacky Wishes!

Royal Sweets
By Helen Perelman

Book 1: *A Royal Rescue*
Book 2: *Sugar Secrets*
Book 3: *Stolen Jewels*
Book 4: *The Marshmallow Ghost*
Book 5: *Chocolate Challenge*

A Miss Mallard Mystery
By Robert Quackenbush

Dig to Disaster
Texas Trail to Calamity
Express Train to Trouble
Stairway to Doom
Bicycle to Treachery
Gondola to Danger
Surfboard to Peril
Taxi to Intrigue

Little Goddess Girls
By Joan Holub and Suzanne Williams

Book 1: *Athena & the Magic Land*
Book 2: *Persephone & the Giant Flowers*
Book 3: *Aphrodite & the Gold Apple*
Book 4: *Artemis & the Awesome Animals*
Book 5: *Athena & the Island Enchantress*
Book 6: *Persephone & the Evil King*

Little GODDESS Girls

Aphrodite & the Magical Box

JOAN HOLUB & SUZANNE WILLIAMS

ALADDIN QUIX

Simon & Schuster Children's Publishing Division

1230 Avenue of the Americas, New York, New York 10020

First Aladdin QUIX hardcover edition May 2021

Text copyright © 2021 by Joan Holub and Suzanne Williams

Illustrations copyright © 2021 by Yuyi Chen

Also available in an Aladdin QUIX paperback edition.

All rights reserved, including the right of reproduction in whole or in part in any form.

ALADDIN and the related marks and colophon are trademarks of Simon & Schuster, Inc.

For information about special discounts for bulk purchases, please contact Simon & Schuster Special Sales at 1-866-506-1949 or business@simonandschuster.com.

The Simon & Schuster Speakers Bureau can bring authors to your live event. For more information or to book an event contact the Simon & Schuster Speakers Bureau at 1-866-248-3049 or visit our website at www.simonspeakers.com.

Designed by Tiara Iandiorio

The illustrations for this book were rendered digitally.

The text of this book was set in Archer Medium.

Manufactured in the United States of America 0421 LAK

2 4 6 8 10 9 7 5 3 1

Library of Congress Control Number 2020951387

ISBN 978-1-5344-7966-1 (hc)

ISBN 978-1-5344-7965-4 (pbk)

ISBN 978-1-5344-7967-8 (eBook)

Cast of Characters

Aphrodite (af•row•DIE•tee): Golden-haired Greek goddess of love and beauty

Athena (uh•THEE•nuh): Brown-haired Greek goddess of wisdom

Persephone (purr•SEFF•uh•nee): Red-haired Greek goddess of plants and flowers

Artemis (AR•tuh•miss): Black-haired Greek goddess of hunting and animals

Oliver (AH•liv•er): Athena's puppy

Hestia (HESS•tee•uh): A small, winged Greek goddess

Zeus (ZOOSS): Most powerful of the Greek gods, who lives in Sparkle City and can grant wishes

Prometheus (pro•MEE•thee•us): A talking carrot from Veggie-Boo-Boo

Pandora (pan•DOR•uh): A very curious talking box

Veggies (VEJ•eez): Talking vegetables in Veggie-Boo-Boo

Head Lettuce (HED LET•us): The mayor of Veggie-Boo-Boo

Bad-Bads: Purple troublemaking bees

Hope (HOHP): Small butterfly fairy who makes others feel hopeful

Contents

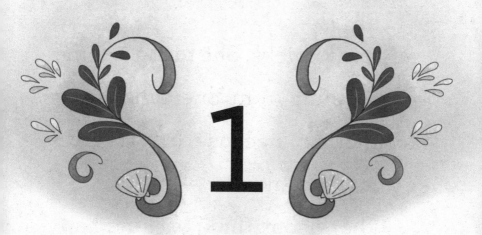

Something Exciting

Aphrodite flipped her long golden hair over her shoulder. Then she stepped onto the Hello Brick Road. This road went through a magical land named **Mount Olympus**. The road was built with orange, blue, and pink bricks. She made a game of hopping from one pink brick to another. Because her favorite color was pink!

"I hope something exciting happens soon," she called to the girls walking behind her. They were her three best friends, **Athena**, **Persephone**, and **Artemis**. The four of them had just gotten back from visiting an island across the sea. There, they'd saved a queen from an evil spell. Talk about exciting!

"Me too," said brown-haired

Athena. A strange storm had blown her to this magic land from her faraway home not long ago. Now she was back for a second visit. She wore a pair of magic winged sandals, and with a click of her heels, they could bring her from her home to Mount Olympus. Whenever she wanted! Since Aphrodite and the other girls all lived here, that worked out great. **"Woof! Woof!"** barked Athena's cute little white dog. His name was **Oliver**. Athena had met him on her first visit and he'd become her pet.

"Oliver is saying 'Me three,'" said Athena. "He wants a new adventure too."

"Me four," said Persephone. She loved plants. Real leaves and flowers grew from her dress and from her curly red hair.

"Me five," agreed Artemis. She wore her hair in a long black braid and always carried a bow and arrows.

During the four girls' adventures

together, they'd met a tiny flying goddess. Her name was **Hestia**. She had told them something amazing: they were all **goddess girls**! If they found a new adventure today, maybe it would give them a chance to use some of their new goddess girl powers!

Just then, Aphrodite noticed a special pink brick near her foot. Unlike the others on the road, it was glittery. Before she could show it to her friends, something exciting *did* happen.

The biggest carrot she'd ever seen came racing up the road toward them. He was about three feet tall. In one hand, he held a torch with a fire burning at its top end.

Persephone giggled at the strange sight. "Maybe he's running away from a giant hungry rabbit," she said.

When the carrot reached them, he

pushed Aphrodite out of his way.

"Oops!" She stumbled back-ward. "**Hey! That was not very nice**, *you . . .* *rot . . . er . . .* raw *carrot*." Aphrodite had been going to say *"you* rotten *carrot."* But she'd caught herself just in time.

She used to say whatever words came into her head. And sometimes that hurt people's feelings or made trouble. However, **Zeus**, the god boy ruler of Mount Olympus, had given her a gift. It was the twinkly crown she wore atop her head. It reminded her to think before she spoke. Her friends had been given gifts too. Gifts that helped them in times of trouble.

The big carrot didn't say he was sorry. Instead, he said, "My name is **Prometheus** Carrot." Then he tapped the bottom end of his torch on the glittery pink brick. *Tap. Tap. Tap.*

Rumble. Rumble. Rumble. Suddenly, a metal closet shot up through the bricks to sit on the road! It stood a few feet taller than the girls. There was a big face above its closed front door.

"Where to?" the face asked the carrot.

"**Veggie-Boo-Boo**!" shouted the carrot.

The door slid open. Still holding his torch, the carrot leaped into the closet. Then he poked a finger at the closet's front wall.

"I think that must be an elevator," Athena whispered to her friends. She was super smart. "And that carrot just pushed one of its buttons."

"Right you are," the elevator told her. Its door slid closed. "Going down. *Beep-beep!*"

"Wait!" called Aphrodite.

But the elevator didn't wait. It zoomed down through the bricks. Then the bricks moved back into place. Now the road looked like before!

Artemis cocked her head. "How cool, or maybe weird, was that?"

"Very," said Aphrodite. "But we wanted an adventure, right?" She bent and knocked on the glittery pink brick. "Come back, elevator!" she called to it. But nothing happened. She tried a few more times.

Knock. Knock. Knock. Still nothing.

Then she spied the shiny silver cane Persephone was holding. Persephone had gotten it from a king on the island they'd just come from. It was magic, but they didn't know what all it could do.

"Try tapping this glittery brick with your cane," suggested Aphrodite.

"And tap three times like that carrot did," added Athena.

Persephone nodded. *Tap. Tap. Tap.*

When the girls heard a rumble, they all jumped back. Just in time! The elevator shot up again.

"Where to?" its face-door asked them. They stared at one another, unsure.

"Um . . . Veggie-Boo-Boo?" Aphrodite asked the others.

They all nodded in agreement. So she repeated the silly words to the elevator.

Whoosh! Its door opened.

2

The Mystery Box

The four girls all looked into the elevator. It was empty. That carrot and his torch were gone.

"Do we dare get in it?" whispered Persephone to her friends.

"Yes!" voted Artemis. She

used to be scared of everything. But Zeus had given her a ruby heart necklace. It reminded her that her own heart was brave whenever she felt afraid. She stepped inside the elevator. Aphrodite, Persephone, and Athena, who carried Oliver in her arms, did too.

Out of the corner of her eye, Aphrodite thought she saw something roll inside with them. It looked sort of like a light blue two-layer cake. She looked around. But there was nothing on the elevator's floor except everyone's feet. She decided it must have been her imagination.

The girls waited inside the elevator for a few moments. But nothing happened.

"Why isn't it moving?" Artemis wondered.

"I can't go anywhere until you push a button," the elevator explained.

"Oh," said Aphrodite. Just then, they noticed the row of three large buttons on the elevator's front wall. Each had writing beside it:

Land 1: Veggie-Boo-Boo

Land 2: Peek-a-Boo-Boo

Land 3: Dragon-Boo-Boo

"Everyone still want to go to Veggie-Boo-Boo?" Athena asked.

Before the goddess girls could decide, a small voice spoke from above. "That's a silly question!"

Looking up, they gasped. Because those four words had come from a round wooden box. A box that could talk! It was light blue and about ten inches from side to side. Like the carrot, it had legs, arms, and a face. And it stood on the elevator's **ceiling**, hanging upside down.

This must be the thing I thought I saw roll into the elevator with us! Aphrodite realized.

The box quickly rolled across the ceiling and halfway down the front wall. It stopped beside the three buttons. It grinned over at the girls. "Why push only one button when you can push them all?" it said. Then the box did exactly that. **Whoosh!** The elevator door closed. They zoomed down.

The box ran down to the floor. Then it rolled around the girls' feet.

It came to a stop by Persephone's silver cane. "Is that a bat?" it asked her. "Are you a baseball player?"

Without waiting for a reply, it went on. "Why do you carry a bow and arrows?" it asked Artemis.

"And where did you get that

crown?" it asked Aphrodite.

"Or those winged shoes?" it asked Athena.

Oliver barked loudly at the box. **"Woof! Woof!"**

The box's eyes went wide. "You don't bite, do you?" it asked.

Before anyone could say a word, the box said, "I'm **Pandora**, by the way. Pandora Box to be exact."

Quickly, before Pandora could go on, Aphrodite said, "I'm Aphrodite. And these are my friends, Athena, Artemis, and Persephone."

"And my dog's name is Oliver," Athena added. "Don't worry. He doesn't bite."

"Where do you all come from?" the box asked as it began to roll around again. "How old are you? What are your favorite games?"

That box asked more questions than anyone Aphrodite had ever met! Not that she'd met any other talking boxes before.

While its back was toward her, Aphrodite noticed something. "Did you know there are words on your back?" she asked Pandora.

"Huh? No! Really?" The box began jumping around, trying to look at its back. "I can't see them. Will you read them to me?"

Aphrodite nodded. "The words say, 'Do not open this box.'"

Pandora's eyes got bigger.

"**What?** You mean there's a way to open me?"

"Well, you do have a lid. Your face is on it," said Athena.

"I do? I wonder what's inside me. Maybe snacks? Or jewels?" Pandora's hands began tugging at her lid. "*Oof! Erg!* Why won't it come off?"

Just then the elevator stopped. Its door opened. "Welcome to the Land of Veggie-Boo-Boo!" it said.

3

Veggie-Boo-Boo

The goddess girls, Oliver, and Pandora stepped out into a beautiful garden. Lettuce, cucumbers, and **broccoli** grew here in neat rows. Bell pepper and **artichoke** plants, too. Green beans and peas hung from vines. And the girls could also see the green tops of carrots, onions, and potatoes. Those were root vegetables that grew underground.

Hearing the elevator door slide shut behind them, Aphrodite called to it over her shoulder. "You'll come back for us?"

"Of course. Just tap the special pink brick three times and I will return." The elevator disappeared.

Huh? thought Aphrodite. But the Hello Brick Road was

somewhere up above them! Before Aphrodite could worry, she saw the glittery pink brick. It lay in the grass nearby. It must have traveled there by magic!

She quickly caught up to her friends. They were wandering among the vegetables in the garden.

"**Wow!** I like this new land. A lot." Persephone was saying.

Artemis grinned at her. "Of course you do, goddess girl of plants!"

Throughout the garden, baby vegetables were still growing. But some newly grown-up vegetables pulled themselves out of the dirt! Other grown-ups leaped from vines or dropped from bushes to walk around. Aphrodite eyed the carrots, but she didn't see Prometheus Carrot.

Some of the grown-up **Veggies** came toward the girls. "Hellooo! Welcome to Veggie-Boo-Boo," they greeted.

A huge ball of lettuce stepped

forward. "I am **Head Lettuce**, the mayor of this land," it announced.

Artemis pointed to herself and her friends. "We are goddess girls," she told the mayor.

Oliver began wiggling in Athena's arms. When she set him down, he ran over to sniff a nearby patch of dead grass.

"Why is that grass black?" the **curious** Pandora piped up. "And why does it smell like smoke?"

"Looks like a small fire burned the grass," said Athena.

Aphrodite blinked. "Fire? Like maybe from a *torch*?"

"Yes. How did you guess?" asked Head Lettuce.

"The fire was a pretty orange and yellow color," said a broccoli stalk, before Aphrodite could reply.

"But we didn't know it would be hot," added a plump potato.

"Super hot," said a little peapod that was still growing on its vine.

"Prometheus Carrot brought it here as a present," said a red bell pepper. "He said fire is good for cooking things to eat!"

The Veggies laughed.

"Silly Prometheus!" said a cucumber. "Veggies never cook. Or eat. We only need sun, rain, and soil to grow healthy and strong."

"We told Prometheus to take his torch away," said an artichoke.

"Stealing fire from Mount Olympus was a big boo-boo," said Head Lettuce.

Hearing this, the goddess girls' eyes went wide.

"He stole it?" said Aphrodite.

The Veggies nodded sadly. "Big bad boo-boo. Zeus would not like it," they said.

"Hmm. Zeus. Where do I know that name from?" said Pandora.

"Zeus rules Mount Olympus from atop **Thunderbolt Tower** in Sparkle City," Athena told her.

The young peapod pointed to Pandora. "His name is written on your back. In tiny letters under DO NOT OPEN THIS BOX, it says ZEUS'S ORDERS."

"Whoa!" said Aphrodite. "You're right! I didn't notice those last two words before."

"Hey! No nibbling!" a cucumber suddenly yelled.

Everyone looked over to see that Oliver was sniffing at a frowning cucumber.

"No, Oliver!" Athena **scolded**. She went over and picked him up.

"His name is Olive?" asked Mayor Head Lettuce. "Olives don't belong in Veggie-Boo-Boo!"

"That's right. Olives are fruit!" yelled a grumpy green bean. "Get that hairy fruit out of here!"

"He's not a fruit," said Athena. "He's a dog. And his name is Oliver, not Olive."

"So did he grow on a *dog*wood tree? Red berries do. And they are fruit," said an angry artichoke.

"They aren't fruit that anyone would eat, though," said Athena.

"The berries might be poisonous."

"Mmm," said Aphrodite. "I could really go for a big bowl of strawberries right now."

The Veggies all gasped. "You eat *fruit*?"

"Well, sure," said Aphrodite. "Vegetables, too." Then, realizing her mistake, she added, "But only the kind that can't walk or talk."

"Hmph! Maybe we should gobble *you* instead," said Mayor Head Lettuce. "Quick! Grab them!"

The Veggies closed in on the girls.

"Run!" Persephone yelled.

The four friends, Oliver, and Pandora Box ran (or rolled) for their lives. The Veggies chased after them, but soon fell far behind.

As they reached the elevator pick-up spot, Persephone grinned and patted the lucky four-leaf clovers in her hair. "Good thing Zeus gave me these as a gift. They helped us run fast!" Then she tapped her cane on the glittery pink brick. *Tap. Tap. Tap.*

Whoosh! The elevator appeared.

The goddess girls and Pandora leaped inside it. The minute Athena set Oliver on the floor, he and Pandora began playing chase.

"I think we should skip going to the other two lands. I say we return to Mount Olympus now," Artemis said. "Even though Zeus gave me the gift of bravery, I'm worried there could be more danger ahead."

"Yeah, maybe you're right," said Aphrodite. She studied the elevator's buttons closely. "Why isn't there a button for Mount

Olympus?" she asked the elevator.

"Pandora pushed all three of my buttons when you first got in, remember?" the elevator explained. "Because of that you must visit all three lands. Only then will a new button appear to return you to Mount Olympus."

Hearing stomping sounds, Aphrodite peeked out the open door. "Here come those Veggies! They look **steamed** . . . I mean **boiling** mad. We'd better go!" She pushed the second button.

The elevator's door whooshed shut in the nick of time. "Going down," it said.

"Do you think we'll find Prometheus Carrot in the next land?" Persephone asked the others.

"Maybe," said Artemis. "Do you think he still has that torch he stole?"

"Probably," said Athena. "I wonder if Zeus knows about it? And where is he?" After he'd given them their goddess girl gifts, he'd **accidentally** flown away in a hot-air balloon.

"You must have seen him," said Aphrodite to Pandora. "He wrote that message on your back, after all. Can you tell us where he is?"

"So many questions. Do you think the answers could be found inside me?" asked Pandora. "Hint. Hint."

Aphrodite folded her arms and shook her head at the little box. "Don't try to trick us into opening your lid. We won't. Not until we meet Zeus again and ask him if it's okay."

"Oh, c'mon," begged Pandora. "What if it's clues to using your goddess girl powers?"

"That would be great. But sorry, no deal," said Athena.

"Agreed," the other three girls said at the same time.

Just then, the elevator stopped. Its door opened. "Welcome to the Land of **Peek-a-Boo-Boo**! Out you go!" it announced.

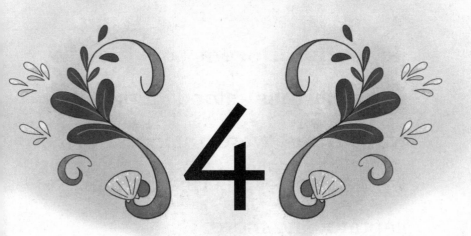

Peek-a-Boo-Boo

Everyone stepped off the elevator.

"Wow!" said Aphrodite, looking around.

They'd landed inside a huge fancy white room! It looked like a Greek temple, with tall stone

columns. Dozens of life-size gray **statues** stood along the walls. There were unicorns, trolls, winged horses, mermaids, a pirate captain, and more.

Whoosh! The door slid shut behind them. The elevator disappeared, leaving only the glittery pink brick on the room's floor.

Suddenly, the stone statues started wiggling. They began jumping up and down. *Hee-hee! Ha-ha!* They were laughing! Slowly, they began turning from gray to pink. The more they laughed, the pinker they got.

"Pink! My favorite color," said Aphrodite. "So far, I kind of like this land."

"Stop tickling us!" begged the statues between laughs.

"They act like they're being tickled pink," said Athena. "That's an old saying for when someone's laughing really hard."

"But I don't see anyone tickling them, do you?" Artemis asked.

The girls all shook their heads.

Wagging his tail in excitement, Oliver ran across the room. He began barking and bounding around the statues. **Click!** Out of nowhere, a group of walking, talking babies appeared beside the statues. The babies wore pajamas. Glowing **Binkys** on long stretchy cords were clipped to their pj's.

"Where did those babies come from?" Pandora asked in surprise.

Hearing her, the babies left the statues to gather around the goddess girls. At once, the statues stopped laughing and wiggling. They turned gray again.

The babies put their hands over their eyes. Then they took them off to look at the girls.

"**Peek-a-Boo-Boo!** We see you!" they chirped.

"Um, hello. We see you, too," Aphrodite replied.

"We are Peek-a-Boo-Boo Babies. Want to play hide-and-seek with us?" asked a baby who was wearing striped pj's.

"Well, okay," Athena said.

"Yeah, I guess we could," said Persephone.

"These are the rules," said a baby in flowered pj's. "You go hide. Then if we find you, we win."

"What if you *can't* find us?" asked Pandora.

"Then, we win anyway," the babies said together. "Either way, guess what? You get tickles!"

"That's sort of cheating," Aphrodite told them in a kind voice.

"What does cheating mean?" asked the baby in flowered pj's.

The goddess girls looked at one another. "Those babies remind me of that evil king we saved the queen from in our last adventure," Artemis said to her friends. "He also liked games, but only if he won them. The babies' rules will make sure they win too."

"They're just babies," said Athena. "They don't know any better."

Aphrodite wasn't so sure. These

babies didn't really act like any babies she knew!

"Arg! 'Tis a terrible game," a nearby pirate statue warned the four girls. "Don't ye play it."

Pandora spun around three times, then asked, "Why do you say that?"

"Unlike you, statues like to stand still," said a troll statue. "We're not good hiders because we're slow and stiff."

A mermaid statue nodded. "When they play with us, the

babies *always* win. Then they tickle us until we turn pink."

"But we aren't slow. We can outrun a bunch of babies. Let's play," said Artemis.

"Okay, close your eyes and count to ten," Aphrodite told the babies.

The Peek-a-Boo-Boos giggled. "We can't count. Just go hide. Now."

The babies put their Binkys into their mouths. **Click!** This made the babies disappear! "Peek-a-Boo-Boo! We see you. But now you can't see us!"

"No fair. That really *is* cheating!" said Aphrodite.

"Yeah," said Athena.

"How can we hide from you if we can't see you?" Pandora asked the babies.

"Right. You could be peeking at us from anywhere," said Persephone.

The babies giggled. "Come on. **Just play!**" they called out.

"Those babies don't understand fairness at all," Artemis grumbled.

"We did try to warn you," a

unicorn statue told the girls. "Prometheus Carrot was here just before you, and the babies made him play too."

The goddess girls looked at the statue in surprise. "That carrot was here?" asked Athena. The statues nodded.

"He laughed so hard from tickles that he almost blew out his torch," said a second troll statue.

"Where is he now?" asked Aphrodite.

"He decided babies and statues

didn't need fire. So he gave up and left," said a third troll.

Just then, the **invisible** babies yelled, **"Gotcha!"** They began tickling the goddess girls, Pandora, and Oliver.

"Hee-hee! Ha-ha!" Soon,

they were all laughing so hard, they were turning pink!

At first the statues seemed pleased the babies had turned their attention to the visitors. But now they began to frown.

"Arg!" the pirate statue grumbled unhappily. "Have ye babies forgotten about us?"

The tickling stopped. Right away, the pink color began to fade from the goddess girls.

The babies all pulled their Binkys out from their mouths.

Everyone could see them again!

"You mean you really want to play our game?" the baby wearing striped pj's asked the statues.

The statues all nodded.

"But you always tell us to stop our tickles," said the baby wearing pj's covered with hearts.

"Well, we didn't know we liked them till now," said the unicorn. "When we weren't playing, we were missing out on the fun."

The goddess girls grinned. Then, while the babies and statues were still talking, they sneaked away. Oliver and Pandora, too.

Behind them, the statues began giggling. They were being tickled pink again!

When the goddess girls came to the glittery pink brick, Persephone reached out with her cane. **_Tap. Tap. Tap._** Right away the elevator arrived. As soon as all were inside, its door slid shut. They pushed the last button. Then the elevator zoomed everyone down to land number three.

5

Dragon-Boo-Boo

Minutes later, the elevator door opened. They were inside a cave!

"Here we are. The Land of **Dragon-Boo-Boo**," the elevator told the goddess girls.

Then Athena pointed at Oliver.

"Sit. Stay. I want you to wait for us in the elevator where it's safe."

Oliver sat. He stayed. But he did not look happy!

Athena patted him on the head. "Don't worry," she said kindly. "We shouldn't be gone long."

Pandora did cartwheels around him. "I'll miss you. Will you miss me?" the box asked over and over.

At last the goddess girls and Pandora left the elevator. The cave was huge. So huge they couldn't see all the way up to its ceiling.

Suddenly they heard snores and snuffles and growls. **Yikes!** They ran back inside the elevator.

"Okay. Been there. Done that," Aphrodite told it. "We're ready to return to Mount Olympus now."

"No shortcuts," the elevator huffed. "Just *going* to a land isn't the same as a true visit. You have to **explore** some. After, just tap the glittery brick to call me back."

"But—" began Aphrodite.

"Out!" the elevator told

them. "I'll watch over your dog while you're gone, no problem."

The goddess girls and Pandora got out again. **Whoosh!** The door slid shut and the elevator disappeared into the ground.

As they walked inside the cave, Aphrodite rubbed her hands together. "It's very cold in here."

Artemis nodded. "Like winter."

"Good thing Veggie-Boo-Boo Land isn't this cold and gloomy. The Veggies wouldn't grow well," said Persephone.

Just then they heard a super loud growl.

"Shh!" said Athena. "Let's be quiet, just in case—"

But it was too late. "Hey!" Pandora called out. "Anybody home?"

The four goddess girls groaned. Seconds later they heard wings flapping. And more growls. And then they smelled smoke.

"Uh-oh," said Aphrodite. She pointed up toward the ceiling.

Three dragons were flying in a circle overhead! They must have been up there watching her and her friends the whole time.

"Cave cold," said the red dragon.

"Fire warm," said the yellow dragon.

"We make fire," said the green dragon. **"Ready, set, go!"**

Snort! Snort! Snort! Orange fire flashed out of their noses!

Athena gasped. "Fire-breathing dragons!"

"At least it is warmer in here now," Persephone noted.

The red dragon nodded. "Yes. Fire make cave cozy."

"Cozy for playing ball game," said the yellow dragon.

"Wanna play too?" asked the green dragon.

"No, thanks!" the goddess girls all said. The last game they'd played had just caused trouble!

But Pandora couldn't control her curiosity. "How do you play?"

"Don't ask!" a voice called out. It was Prometheus Carrot! His torch shone brightly as he came toward them from somewhere deep in the cave.

Before he could reach the girls, the dragons explained their game.

"You all run around cave really fast," the red dragon said.

"While we fly after you," the yellow dragon added.

"And breathe fireballs at you," said the green dragon. "Sounds fun, right?"

"No," said Aphrodite. "Trying not to get hit by fireballs does *not* sound like fun!"

Keeping quiet for once, Pandora rolled to one side of the cave to hide. Fire could be very dangerous for a wooden box!

"Well, it's fun for *us*," said the red dragon. All three dragons smiled, showing sharp teeth.

Prometheus Carrot caught up to the girls. "It's my fault," he said. "I stole fire from Mount Olympus."

"We know," said Athena.

"So did

you give these dragons their fire breath?" asked Aphrodite.

"Um, yeah," Prometheus told the girls. "I'd once heard Zeus say fire is a game. I like games. Well, *most* games, anyway." Everyone glanced up at the dragons.

The dragons circling overhead grinned. "Ready for fireball?" they asked, grinning.

"Not really," said Persephone.

Prometheus sighed. "While Zeus was away from Mount Olympus I stole this torch. And I brought fire to the three Lands of Boo-Boo."

"That was a big boo-boo!" yelled a new voice from overhead. "One that caused boo-boos in the Lands of Boo-Boo!"

Everyone looked up as a hot-air balloon floated into the cave. A black-haired boy stood in the big basket that hung from the bottom of it. He wore a **tunic** and there was a shiny thunderbolt on his belt.

"It's Zeus!" Athena exclaimed.

"I never said fire was a *game*!" Zeus called down to the carrot. "I said another *name* for fire is *flame*."

The carrot hunched his shoulders. "Oops. I guess I did make a big boo-boo. Sorry."

The dragons swooped toward the balloon for a better look. **"Not too close!"** Zeus warned, waving his arms. "Your sharp teeth might pop it!"

The dragons whipped around in surprise. The tip of the green dragon's tail swished down to the floor. It knocked Pandora from her hiding place. Her lid flew off. **Pandora Box was open!**

6

Hope

Five tiny purple dots flew out of the open box. They quickly grew to the size of bees. They buzzed around the dragons.

"We are the **Bad-Bads**," they said. And then they began to sing this song:

"We like to be naughty.

We like to be bad.

We like to cause trouble,

and make others mad."

"Their kind of trouble sounds way worse than tickle trouble," said Athena.

The dragons seemed to agree. "Let's g-get out of h-here!" the red dragon said to the other two. Flapping their wings, the three of them zoomed deeper into their cave and out of sight.

While Zeus was busy trying to land his balloon, the Bad-Bads flew out of the cave. "We're off to make trouble in the lands of the Boo-Boos!" they called back.

"**Hey!** What's going on? Why is my backside cold?" asked Pandora. The box was in two pieces now. Its bottom half lay on the ground near Aphrodite. Its lid-face half was running around the cave yelling.

Aphrodite picked up the yelling lid-face as it ran by. She set it on the bottom half. **_Snap!_** She put Pandora Box together again.

Pandora smiled at her. "Thanks!"

Zeus let the hot air out of his balloon and brought it down to the ground. Then

he climbed out of the basket. He pointed a finger at Prometheus Carrot.

"Stealing is a no-no," Zeus told the big carrot. "When you stole fire from Sparkle City, you set off a magical **punishment**."

"Huh? You mean those Bad-Bads?" asked Pandora.

Zeus nodded. "From now on the Bad-Bads will live in the Boo-Boo Lands. They'll make plenty of trouble, but don't worry. There will also be help for those bothered by their trouble-making."

Just then, a sparkly light began to blink near the balloon. A tiny butterfly lady appeared. "Did someone say trouble?" she asked.

"Hestia?" asked Artemis. "No, wait. You're not Hestia. She glows."

"I'm her fairy friend," the butterfly lady replied. "My name is **Hope**. In troubled times, I go where I'm needed."

"So you came because the Bad-Bads are bringing trouble

to the Boo-Boo Lands?" asked Prometheus.

The butterfly fairy smiled. "That's right. I'm here to bring hope to the three lands." She looked at Pandora Box. "I may need a helper, though."

"You mean me?" Pandora asked "What can I do?"

"You're good at asking questions," said Hope. "Questions can get others to talk about their troubles. Which can make them feel better."

"So you want me to ask Boo-Boo-Landers about their troubles?" said Pandora. She looked excited about the idea.

Hope nodded. "Yes. And maybe between us, we can help them feel happier and more *hopeful.*"

"**Yay!** Count me in," said Pandora.

Hope swooped down. Pandora Box reached up. A magical light flashed when they held hands. Then the two of them flew off to follow the Bad-Bads.

"Looks like our adventure has come to a happy ending," said Aphrodite. Her friends smiled.

"Glad to hear it! Now, I've been away from Sparkle City for too long," said Zeus. "I need to get back to see how things are going."

He held out a hand for the torch. Prometheus gave it to him. Zeus used the flame's heat to power up his hot-air balloon.

Then Zeus turned to the four goddess girls. "I'll take this carrot home to Veggie-Boo-Boo. Take the elevator back to Mount Olympus. From there, follow the Hello Brick Road to meet me in Sparkle City."

He and Prometheus Carrot hopped into the basket. As the balloon rose higher, Zeus waved goodbye. "See you all in Sparkle

City for the pet contest!" he shouted to the girls.

They looked at him in surprise and excitement.

"What pet contest?" Artemis called up to him. She loved animals!

But Zeus's balloon had already floated out of the cave.

Persephone quickly tapped the glittery pink brick. This time, there was only one button on the elevator's wall when it came. The button read: MOUNT OLYMPUS.

Within minutes the girls and

Oliver were back on the Hello Brick Road. Ahead of them, the top of Mount Olympus shimmered with the rainbow sparkles of Sparkle City.

"Speaking of hope, I *hope* we make it in time for that pet contest!" joked Aphrodite.

The goddess girls all laughed. Then they linked arms. With Oliver trotting along beside them, they began to merrily skip toward Sparkle City.

Word List

accidentally (ax•ih•DENT•lee): By mistake

artichoke (AR•tih•choak): A green vegetable that looks like a prickly bush

Binkys (BINK•eez): Rubber or plastic nipples babies suck on

broccoli (BRAHK•uh•lee): A green vegetable that looks like a tree

ceiling (SEE•ling): The inside top of a room

columns (KAH•luhmz): Tall posts

curious (KYOOR•ee•us): Interested in learning more about something

Dragon-Boo-Boo (DRAG•un•bu•bu):
A cave of dragons

explore (ex•PLOOR): Travel
through a new place to learn about it

invisible (in•VIH•zih•bull):
Something you can't see

mortal (MOR•tuhl): A human

**Mount Olympus (MOWNT
Oh•LIHM•puhs):** Tallest mountain
in Greece

Peek-a-Boo-Boo (PEEK•uh•bu•bu):
A land of babies and statues

punishment (PUN•ish•ment):
Something not fun done to

someone because they did wrong

scolded (SKOLL•did): Told someone they've done something bad or wrong

statues (STA•chooz): Figures of a person or animal made of stone

Thunderbolt Tower (THUN•der•bolt TOW•er): Where Zeus lives in Sparkle City

tunic (TOO•nihk): A knee-length shirt

Veggie-Boo-Boo (VEJ•ee•bu•bu): A land of talking vegetables

Questions

1. Which of the three lands did you enjoy most? Why?
2. If you could meet any of the creatures, in what silly ways could you greet them?
3. If you had a magic elevator, where would you like it to take you?
4. What questions could you ask a new friend to get to know them?
5. What top three things do you hope will happen in your life? How will you make them happen?

Authors' Note

This book is based on a Greek myth called "Pandora's Box." It starts when a boy named Prometheus steals fire from the Greek gods. He gives the fire to his **mortal** friends, which makes Zeus mad. To punish mortals, Zeus sends a box to a curious girl named Pandora. She is not supposed to open it, but she can't stop herself! Turns out the box is full of troubles, but hope saves the day.

We hope you enjoy reading all the Little Goddess Girls books!

—*Joan Holub and Suzanne Williams*